Owen and the Onion

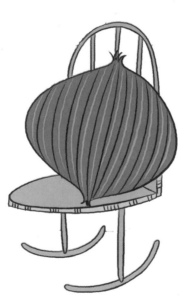

Owen and the Onion

Maudie Smith

Illustrated by Becka Moor

Orion
Children's Books

First published in Great Britain in 2015
by Orion Children's Books
an imprint of Hachette Children's Group
and published by Hodder and Stoughton Limited
Orion House
5 Upper St Martin's Lane
London WC2H 9EA
An Hachette UK Company

1 3 5 7 9 10 8 6 4 2

Text © Maudie Smith 2015
Illustrations © Becka Moor 2015

ISBN 978 1 4440 1423 5

A catalogue record for this book
is available from the British Library.

Printed and bound in China

www.orionbooks.co.uk

For Lucy Lark

Contents

Chapter One

Owen lived on an onion farm.

Owen loved helping his dad with the onions. He helped plant the onions. He helped with the weeding and the watering.

At the end of summer, when the
onions were brown and perfectly ripe,
he helped pick them and pack them
in baskets.

Then Owen and his dad took the
onion baskets down the hill to the
village.

The villagers loved the onions. When winter came, and there wasn't much else to eat, they used them to make soup. The onion soup filled and warmed their grumbling stomachs, and it tasted delicious.

HOORAY FOR ONIONS!

YUMMY YUMMY!

LOOK, MUM! THE ONIONS ARE COMING!

Once they had delivered the onions, Owen and his dad went home to relax. But before they put their feet up, they always remembered to put up the NO OGRES sign.

NO OGRES HERE, THANK YOU! THIS IS AN OGRE-FREE VILLAGE. OGRES KEEP OUT!

Ogres often came down from
the mountains in winter. No one
wanted them coming into the village,
throwing their weight around.

Luckily, ogres were very good at
reading signs.

One spring morning, Owen's dad
opened a letter from the King.
   "Oh, dear!" he said.
   "What is it?" said Owen.

"I've been summoned to the palace. The King has a new hobby. Onion-growing! He wants me to teach him how to do it."

"That's fantastic!" said Owen.

"Hmm," said Owen's dad. "I'm not so sure. I've met the King before. But there's nothing for it. I'll have to go.

You'll have to look after the onions this year, Owen. Do you think you can manage that?"

"You bet I can!" said Owen.

Chapter Two

Everything went well at first.

Owen prepared the ground as usual.

He planted the onions as usual.

As the onions began to grow, he weeded and watered them as usual.

But then Owen noticed that one of the onions was different from the rest. It was much bigger. It smelled different too. Sweeter, and stronger.

Owen took one sniff of that
onion and his head began to spin.
He sniffed it again, and again, until
he couldn't stop sniffing it.

Owen spent more and more time with the unusual onion. He tended it and he watered it, and he kept on smelling its wonderful smell.

He forgot all about the other onions.

At last, when the onion was as big as his head, Owen picked it.

Owen didn't want to share the onion with anyone. He hid it away in the farmhouse.

How Owen loved that onion!
He dusted it as if it was a vase.
He stroked it as if it was a cat. He
cuddled it as if it was a baby.

The onion must have liked all
the attention Owen was giving it,
because it carried on growing.

Owen didn't pick his other onions.
They stayed in the ground. When
the autumn rains came, the other
onions rotted away.

Owen didn't notice. He only had eyes, and nose, for one onion now.

Chapter Three

Winter came.

Owen's onion had grown even bigger, but the villagers' stomachs had grown much smaller. They climbed the hill and knocked on Owen's door.

"Owen!" they called. "We're starving! We need to make some soup. Do you have any onions?"

"No!" Owen lied. "There are no onions here! Go away and leave me alone!"

Owen didn't care about the villagers. He only cared about his onion.

Owen was so busy with his onion, he didn't notice the ogre thudding past on his way to the village.

Ogres were always grumpy in winter, but this ogre was grumpier than most. He was angry because he didn't know how to cry.

"Tell me something sad," he said
to the villagers. "I want to know what
it feels like to have tears streaming
down my cheeks."

The villagers tried to think of the
saddest stories they knew, but they were
so hungry they couldn't think straight.
None of their stories made the ogre cry.

"Do something to hurt me, then!" the ogre demanded. "Make me cry that way!"

The villagers trod on the ogre's toes. They pinched his wrists and poked his cheeks, but they couldn't make any tears fall from his eyes.

"Useless!" shouted the ogre.
He punched holes in sheds. He bit the tops off trees and he stamped the water out of the rivers. He wouldn't leave the village.

Owen didn't even know he was there.

Chapter Four

The ogre rounded the villagers up on the village green.

"If you don't make me cry in one minute," he said, "I'm going to squash you all flat!"

He lifted his foot and he yelled.

That yell was so loud it made
the roof tiles tremble. It scared the
clouds away. And it rustled the skin
of Owen's onion.

Now it wasn't just the ogre who was angry. Owen was angry too.

"Hey, you!" Owen shouted. "Be quiet! You're disturbing my onion!"

The ogre was just about to stamp
on the villagers when,
Snap!
Owen's onion burst through the
walls of the farmhouse.

Owen and the onion went flying
down the hill, onto the village
green.

Owen stood up and took a deep breath of fresh air.

For the first time in a long time he stopped thinking about his onion. He saw what was going on around him.

He saw the villagers, shaking under the ogre's foot. He saw how skinny they had become. He saw how afraid they were.

Owen felt terrible. He hadn't taken any onions to the village. He'd completely forgotten to put up the NO OGRES sign. This was all his fault.

"Stop!" he shouted. "Please stop!"

"Shan't!" the ogre shouted back. "Not unless you can make me cry in the next twenty seconds!"

"I can!" said Owen. "I will!"

"Can't!" scoffed the ogre. "It's impossible. Sad stories don't make me cry. Nor does treading, or pinching, or poking. It can't be done."

He wiggled his tree trunk toes, ready to stamp.

Owen knew he had to think of
something quickly.

He looked at the ogre. He looked
at his village friends. He looked at his
precious onion. And he had an idea.

"Wait!" Owen cried. "I know
what to do!"

Chapter Five

"Before you stamp on these poor people," said Owen, "I want you to squash this onion flat."

"It looks like a very nice onion," said the ogre. "Are you sure you want me to squash it?"

"Quite sure," Owen said.

"All right," grunted the ogre.

"But I don't see what good it can do."

Splotch!

The ogre squashed the onion to mush.

Squelch!

Oh! What a smell came out of that onion!

It was a pong to make your hair wilt, a stink to make your teeth chatter, a stench to make you go weak at the knees.

The ogre put his nose in the onion mush and sniffed. At once his eyes started to sting and to water. Tears as big as pears dripped down his cheeks.

"I'm crying!" he cried. "I'm crying at last!"

The ogre looked at the villagers,
who were still shivering below him.
"Aw, I'm sorry, folks," he said.
"I'm sorry I frightened you."

He picked up the villagers and
put them safely out of the way of his
gigantic feet.

He gave Owen a slobbery kiss.

"I'm a different ogre now, thanks to you," he said, smiling through his tears. And with that, the ogre danced out of the village.

Chapter Six

"Sorry about your onion, Owen," said the villagers. "What shall we do with it now?"

"Make soup, of course!" Owen said. "Eat it at once!"

So the villagers gathered up the onion and used it to make onion soup.

The soup filled and warmed
their grumbling stomachs, and it
tasted delicious. There was enough
for everyone to have seconds, and
thirds, and even fourths.

They were still eating the soup when Owen's dad drove into the village. The villagers rushed up to him.

"Owen's onion has saved our lives!" they cried. "That boy is a wonder!"

"He's a quick learner, all right," said Owen's dad. "Much quicker than the King! I'm proud of you, Owen."

Owen wasn't proud of himself. He was ashamed of the way his onion had made him behave.

Owen's dad patted him on the back. "Well done, son. You can be in charge of the onions next year, too, if you like."

But Owen never wanted to see another onion in his life.

"Thanks, Dad," he said. "But if it's all right with you, I don't want to grow onions next year."

"Really?" said Owen's dad. "What *do* you want to grow, then?"

"Beans!" said Owen.
Because Owen was sure growing beans would be much *much* safer!